BETRAYAL IN THE JUSTICE ALLIANCE

by Ashley Sherer

Ashley Sherer

Front Cover Art by Joslin Bowen
Back Cover Logo by www.fiverr.com/srishet123

Sirens pierced the air as police cars surrounded the First National Bank of Logan City. Four police officers huddled behind a black and white squad car, as a slender, bald, purple-skinned alien walked up from behind them.

"Lieutenant Murphy. I intercepted an emergency call while on patrol. What's the situation?" asked the alien, Janus, as he crouched alongside the officers.

"Janus, I'm glad you're here," answered a muscular officer with a mustache, "Bank robbers attempted to make off with a currency shipment this afternoon. We got lucky though; one teller triggered the silent alarm. Now they've wired up the whole building with explosives and moved all the employees to the back of the bank."

"And their demands?" asked Janus as he furrowed his ridged brow.

"If we don't give them safe passage out, they will kill the hostages and bring the whole building down. They've demanded a chopper with a pilot to come and get them. Can you help us?"

"I can, Lieutenant. Keep your men back."

Janus turned to the bank and walked toward the door. Before he could reach the entrance, a gray and red blur rocketed past him, crashing through the bank doors, and sending shards of glass flying. Within seconds, screams and thumping sounds emanated from inside the bank. As the scene grew quiet, three men wearing black flew out of the bank and landed in a pile in front of the squad car.

"What the hell?" cried the astonished Lieutenant as he walked around the patrol car to check out the three limp bodies hurled from the bank. As he knelt down beside them, the gray and red figure zoomed out of the building.

"Do not be afraid, citizens. It is I, Magnus Superior, here to save the day."

Magnus hovered in the air, gray cape flowing in the wind. His hands were on his hips and his face was turned toward the morning sun.

"Thanks Magnus, but these clowns set

explosives on all the major support columns in the bank. Can you disarm them?" asked the Lieutenant.

A frown fell across Janus' face.

With another rush of air, Magnus Superior sped into the bank. Within seconds, he was back outside holding the explosive devices.

"Turn away good citizens of Logan City. I will detonate these bombs against my indestructible body," said Magnus with a booming voice as he cradled them in his massive, muscular arms.

The police and onlookers ducked down behind the cars parked along the street and covered their heads. Instead of taking cover, Janus looked on disinterested. A cloud of dust enveloped Magnus as a muffled explosion was heard. As he continued to hover in the air, he crossed his arms and looked off into the distance.

"Good citizens, you are now safe, thanks to Magnus Superior."

The crowd of policemen and spectators clapped wildly for their hero as Janus walked off unnoticed.

Later that afternoon, thick acrid smoke poured from a warehouse in the Logan City waterfront district. Sirens filled the air as several firetrucks arrived on the scene and surrounded the burning structure. A tall, muscular, blonde woman dressed in ancient Greek warrior gear towered over the much shorter Logan City fire chief.

"Skylla, I'm glad you're here."

"How bad is it chief?"

"It's as bad as it gets. Come and look at the floor layout," said the chief as he and Skylla walked over to his car where a set of blueprints laid on the hood.

"There are two men trapped in the center of the warehouse and we haven't been able to get to them. I don't even know if they're still alive. Plus, there are four natural gas tanks on the north side of the building. I don't need to tell you what happens if the fire gets to them. We're working with the police to evacuate the area, but it's slow and the fire is spreading quick."

"I'll get those men out, while you concentrate on containing the fire," said Skylla.

"Right. Engines Four and Five get a stream on those windows," yelled the chief into his walkie-talkie.

Just as Skylla crouched to jump into the warehouse, the familiar gray and red blur whizzed by the group and plunged into the inferno. Within seconds, Magnus Superior brought out the two trapped victims and dropped them in front of the startled fire chief and his men.

"Chief, these men will need some medical attention."

"Thanks Magnus, but the warehouse..."

Magnus Superior assumed his familiar hands-on-hips pose as he floated four feet in the air.

"No need to worry, Magnus Superior is here."

"Magnus, I had this covered," argued Skylla.

"I'm sure you thought so, but leave dangerous situations like this to me."

"Why you-" she said when Magnus Superior interrupted and held his hand up, "I will now put out the fire. Please stand back."

Magnus floated over the warehouse and inhaled. As he spun in a circle, he exhaled at supersonic speed. Within seconds, the flames that had threatened the entire structure disappeared. After surveying his work, Magnus flew over and landed beside the fire chief.

"I would suggest you keep your hoses on that building to take care of any hotspots."

"Yes sir, Magnus," said the chief before he pulled out his walkie-talkie and radioed his men, "We need to keep pouring that water on to knock out any hotspots."

"Roger that," came the reply from several of the chief's men.

"Thank you, Magnus," said the Chief.

"You're welcome, good citizen. Skylla can help mop up any remaining problems. Remember, Magnus Superior is always here for you."

Skylla began to protest, but kept quiet as she dug her fingernails into the palms of her hands. Her eyes burned as she watched Magnus Superior turn from the crowd and fly away with a speed that caused a sonic boom.

Early the next morning, a gaunt, pale figure dressed in a dark blue suit rode on his motorcycle through the streets of downtown Logan City. As the Shadow Wraith turned onto Main street, he came upon a large crowd of people clustered at an intersection. He parked his bike and approached two police officers standing behind their patrol car.

"Sergeant, may I be of service?"

"I sure hope so, Shadow Wraith. We've got a man holding a knife to a young kid's throat threatening to kill her."

"Is the girl ok?"

"So far, but this guy must be on something. He

grabbed her from the mall while she was out with her friends. When one of my officers confronted him, he dragged her out here to the middle of the street. We thought it might have been a kidnapping gone bad, but now he's talking about demons and how they won't take his little girl. The thing is she's not his daughter, but he imagines she is. He says he'll kill her first before 'they' destroy her."

"What is his name?"

"At this point we don't know. We're interviewing witnesses to see if they know him or heard him say his name, but we've got nothing."

"Do we know who she is?"

"Yeah, her name is Melissa Markum. She's 13 and according to her friends, has no connection to the man at all."

"I'm going to try to talk to him, unless you object."

"At this point, I'm willing to try anything. The way he's got her in his arms, we can't try to take a shot at him for fear of hitting her."

"I'll go see if I can help," said the Shadow Wraith as he floated through the crowd and positioned himself in the intersection. As he approached, the burly man held his knife tight against the girl's pale, slender neck.

"Demon, don't come any closer or I'll cut her

throat," said the man as he clutched the girl to his chest.

"I didn't do anything to you, please don't," begged Melissa as a small trickle of blood flowed down her neck.

"It will be ok Melissa, I just want to talk to him," said the Shadow Wraith before turning his attention to her captor, "What's your name?"

"Charles," he said as he tightened his grip around the girl.

"Charles, please understand that I'm not a demon and I won't come near. I just want to help. Can we talk?"

"Stay out of my mind, you're trying to trick me."

"Charles, I'm the Shadow Wraith. I help people and I want to help you."

"You can't help me; no one can. They want to take her and I won't let them."

"Who Charles? No one wants to take her. We only want to help."

"The doctors, they want to put me away, but I know what they really want. They want me in the pit where no one ever comes back from. I'll never see her again."

"Charles, the doctors want to help. There is no pit. Charles, if I take you to the doctors and show you there is no pit will you let me?"

"I don't know, I'm just so confused."

"I know, but I want to help and the doctors want to help. Now, will you trust me and let this girl go?"

"I just..."

Charles began to lower his knife when a blur flew over the crowd and struck the man. The force of the blow sent him flying across the road.

Melissa screamed as the Shadow Wraith grabbed her and handed her to one of the nearby police officers.

"Not to worry young one, Magnus Superior is here," he said as he grabbed Charles and twisted his arm behind his back.

The crowd cheered as they saw the man disarmed and the girl would be safe.

"Great job Magnus. This guy here was just going to talk him to death. It takes a real man to take care of business," yelled a man from the crowd.

"Yeah, great job," said a second man.

As if on cue, the crowd erupted in applause.

Magnus rose in the air and declared, "Magnus Superior is always here for you, my people. I am here to save and to serve."

As he flew away,the adoring crowd strained to get one last glance at their hero. While the throng cheered, Shadow Wraith floated away, ignored and unnoticed.

In the evening of the next day, The Moth and
Owl Boy were on patrol when a police dispatch
came over the radio.

"All units near 10th Street and 3rd Avenue,
please proceed to the Szasz office building. We
have reports that the super-villain known as
'The Lamprey' has taken a group of people
hostage on the 7th floor. SWAT will be there in
15 minutes. Do not enter. All units are ordered
to set up a perimeter to contain the situation."

"Hold on, we're going to take care of this
problem permanently," said The Moth as he
pressed the accelerator on The Moth Rocket Car.
Beating the nearest police units to the building,
he pulled into a side street alley.

"How do we get in, through the window?" asked Owl Boy.

"I really get tired of spoon-feeding you. Will you ever 'get it'?"

"Ok, how then?" asked Owl Boy.

"You're over-analyzing it. The Lamprey is already feeding on those idiots up there. We can just walk through the door."

Both men ran into the lobby and bounded up the stairs. In record time, they were on the seventh floor.

"How do we know which room they're in?" asked Owl Boy.

A scream from six doors down answered the question. Both men crept down the hall, taking up a position outside the room.

"What's the plan, Moth?"

"Just stay out of my way."

"But wait-" said Owl Boy as he outstretched his arms to slow The Moth down.

The Moth ignored his sidekick and kicked the door before he could finish speaking. The flimsy door exploded into a shower of wood shrapnel that sprayed the inside of the apartment. The Moth and Owl Boy rushed in to find limp bodies scattered about the room like wet towels, their skin as white as chalk. The ashen, cadaverous Lamprey stood in the middle of the carnage with his mouth pressed against the latest victim's neck. The force of the suction caused her muscles to twitch and spasm with every ounce of blood that left her body. Her skin was as pale as the victim's on the floor and her body was so weak the Lamprey had to hold her up with his long, white fingers.

"Lamprey, your time is over now," said The Moth.

The Lamprey detached his mouth from the woman's neck as blood dribbled down his chin.

"Moth, I've waited to taste your blood for a long time. I will savor it, like you might savor a fine wine."

The Lamprey had just gotten the last word out of his mouth when he pushed his victim through the air into Owl Boy. As he did, The Moth flexed his powerful leg muscles and sprung into the air. Just as he left the ground, Owl Boy staggered from being hit by the woman and clipped The Moth in his legs. The Moth stumbled, head first into a desk, stunning him. Owl Boy charged the Lamprey, but as he came near, the Lamprey hit him with a spin kick, knocking him to the floor out cold.

"You lose, Moth. I will start by desiccating your protege. I will drink his blood until he is a dried-out husk."

The Moth staggered to his knees and tried to get to Owl Boy. Before he could get there, the Lamprey picked up Owl Boy and placed his mouth on the unconscious sidekick's neck. As he started to drain his newest target's blood, a loud crash was heard from the window.

"Citizens of Logan City, it is I, Magnus Superior here to save you."

The Lamprey dropped Owl Boy and headed toward the door. With his super-speed, Magnus got there first, blocking the Lamprey's escape. The Lamprey threw a right cross into the steel-hard jaw of Magnus Superior, breaking his hand.

"Aaaarrrrgggghhh," the Lamprey cried.

Magnus Superior thumped the Lamprey on his chin, knocking him out and to the floor. He then walked over to Owl Boy and helped him up.

"Are you ok?" asked Magnus.

"I am, but what about The Moth?"

"I'm fine," came the reply from behind both men.

The Moth had gathered his senses and pulled himself up from the ground.

Magnus walked over to him.

"I had this under control, you alien intruder," said The Moth jamming his finger into the chest of Magnus Superior.

"Now, now, Moth. You do a fine job on bank robbers or purse snatchers. For you and your ward's safety, leave the super-powered villains to those with the skill and ability to stop them."

"Why you arrogant, overblown-" said The Moth as he got nose to nose with Magnus.

Before he could finish, Magnus gave a nod and wink and grabbed up the Lamprey as he flew out of the broken window. Owl Boy staggered over to The Moth.

"Don't listen to him, Moth."

The Moth swung the back of his hand into the jaw of Owl Boy.

"Don't you ever tell me what to do. And if you ever get in my way again, I'll park you on the side of the road, permanently."

Without another word, The Moth went out the door with Owl Boy following after him, rubbing his jaw.

Three days later, the Justice Alliance assembled at their headquarters, the space ship Freedom, for their regular weekly meeting.

"You know, I really hate getting together these days," declared Janus as the group walked through the long, gray corridor to the main meeting hall.

"Even the pursuit of justice has to acquiesce to the monument of bureaucracy," responded the Shadow Wraith.

"Instead of whining about this waste of time, why don't you talk less and get it over with," grumbled The Moth.

"Always the people person, aren't you Moth?"

quipped Skylla.

The doors to the meeting hall opened, and the group walked into a pitch black room.

"What's wrong with the lights?" asked Skylla.

"Here, I've got my Moth Light, let me check the panel."

The Moth took the light out of his utility sash and shined it at the control panel by the door.

"Odd, somebody's removed the panel and disconnected a couple of wires," explained The Moth.

While he held the flashlight in his teeth, The Moth connected the two loose wires. As the lights in the room came on, the group saw Magnus Superior seated in the chair at the head of the table.

"A bit melodramatic even for you, don't you think, Magnus?" asked the Shadow Wraith.

"Magnus?" repeated the Shadow Wraith.

The four heroes walked over to the chair where he was seated.

"You've taken this too far Magnus," said Skylla.

"Magnus?" echoed Janus.

"He can't hear you," The Moth shoved his body

forward onto the table revealing a long, silver blade embedded in his back, "because he's dead. Nobody touches anything and don't even think about going anywhere."

"How could anyone stab Magnus?" asked Janus.

"He had one weakness. Exposure to anything made of Zim metal would nullify his powers, but I suspect that one of you already knew that," answered The Moth.

"You're talking like you think that one of us did it," said Skylla.

"You three are the most likely suspects. Who else can get up here? Think about it. Without the code, the bio-scan and the transport device you can't get on this ship. The force field makes it impregnable."

"That's foolish Moth and where do you get off thinking you're in charge. We've all done this before," said Janus as he examined the area around the body.

"I said no one touch anything!" yelled The Moth.

The Moth grabbed Janus and threw him across the room.

With blinding speed, Skylla grabbed The Moth and tossed him to the floor.

"ENOUGH!!!"

The loud cry from the Shadow Wraith stunned everyone in the room and all eyes turned toward his ethereal form.

"For now, I suggest we let The Moth do his work. It is what he is best at, and whether we want to admit it or not, he is better than us."

"And what if he did it?"

Everyone turned to Skylla.

"Then we will deal with him. Not even The Moth can stand against the combined power of the Justice Alliance."

"That's your opinion, dead man. Everyone out of here, I need room to work."

"Call me if you need me, I'm going back to Logan City," said Skylla with a dismissive wave of her hand.

"I don't think so," said The Moth as he pulled a square device from his sash and pressed a small blue button. "I've just activated the force shield on the Freedom. No one leaves until I say they do."

"Why you... what if we're needed?" asked Janus.

"I suggest we contact some of the other heroes and let them know," interjected the Shadow Wraith.

"Good call dead man," said The Moth.

"I will make the call, and Moth?"

"Yeah?"

"I'm not dead, just different."

"Not dead yet anyway," The Moth responded.

The three heroes marched out of the room leaving The Moth to start the investigation. The Shadow Wraith floated toward the communication room while Janus and Skylla stared at the closed meeting door.

"Want some coffee, Janus?"

"I would. Thank you, Skylla."

The two heroes made their way down the main corridor of the Freedom and into the bright yellow and orange break room located beside the ship's galley. Skylla punched the command to make coffee into the ship's automated beverage machine. Within minutes, the coffee poured into a shiny, silver carafe. Once the machine finished, she walked over to where Janus sat and poured the hot, steaming coffee into two white, porcelain mugs. After handing Janus a cup, she sat down across from him.

"Who does The Moth think he is?" asked Janus as he sipped from the cup.

"You know how he is. The Moth won't ever consider the possibility that one of Magnus

Superior's enemies did it. He just won't listen."

"I'm about sick of the barely sane 'detective', Why I..."

Janus' voice trailed off as he noticed The Moth standing by the door to the break room, scowling.

"Something you'd like to say to me, alien?" asked The Moth as he flexed his neck muscles and popped his knuckles.

"No, nothing," replied Janus as he walked past The Moth and down the hall.

"You realize that we're on the same side," offered Skylla.

"I don't know any such thing. I'm on my side and that's the only thing I'm sure of."

"You really are a bastard all the time."

"It's kept me alive."

"It's also kept you alone, except for your ever-devoted sidekick. Now if you'll excuse me," said Skylla as she drank the last of her coffee and walked out of the break room. After she left, The Moth sat down at the now empty table.

"Do you really think you can spy on me, Wraith?"

"I never spy, I only observe. It serves me well,"

came the voice from behind The Moth.

"I don't like it and never did. Did you send the message?" asked The Moth as he turned to face the Shadow Wraith.

"I did. Don't you think that this might be more than you can handle? Even the 'great' Moth might need my assistance," said the Shadow Wraith as he sat down at the table across from The Moth.

"I already have one partner who can barely keep up. I don't need another, so don't get in my way. Remember, I can stop all of you any time I want."

"Like you could stop Magnus Superior?" asked the Shadow Wraith.

"He never forgot it, I suggest you don't either," answered The Moth as he poked the Shadow Wraith in the chest.

The Moth pushed himself away from the table and walked out of the room, leaving the Shadow Wraith to himself. Once in the hall, he marched to the computer room and sat down at a terminal to activate the voice interface.

"Computer, this is The Moth, access code Bravo Delta Six Four Two."

"Access Granted," the metallic voice of the computer responded.

"Have any unauthorized people been on this ship over the last 12 hours?"

"Answer, no one is on the ship."

"Don't you mean there have been no unauthorized people?"

"Answer, there is no one on this ship. There is no one on the ship now and there has not been anyone on the ship for the last 36 hours."

"Computer, run a full scan on the ship. You should find four living beings, plus one corpse," ordered The Moth, anger in his voice rising.

"Answer, scan complete. There is no one on the ship now. No living or non-living beings."

"Computer, how do you explain that I am on the ship asking you these questions?"

"Answer, there is no one on this ship now."

The Moth shook his head and continued, "Computer, please run a full self-diagnostic. Also, please pull up the surveillance video for the main meeting room and adjacent corridors. Display on monitors, 1 and 2."

"Diagnostic started. Unable to comply with video request. There is no video."

"So you've been tampered with," said The Moth.

"Please repeat your query, unable to

understand."

"Nothing computer, disregard last request."

The Moth stood up and headed back to the meeting room. He removed the sheet that had covered Magnus' body and examined the blade still embedded in his back. The silver blade, now stained with dried, dark-red blood, was truly a work of art. Even after examining it with a magnifier, there were no flaws or imperfections to be found. The blade was made of Zim metal as he expected. The problem was that Zim metal was rare and very difficult to work with. Whoever had forged this was a true craftsman. The Moth was left wondering how it would be possible for anyone to stab Magnus. He had superior senses and lightning-fast speed. It just didn't make sense to him. He didn't like Magnus, but why would anyone... His thoughts trailed off, and he smiled to himself. The Moth realized who did it and how it was done. After the revelation hit him, The Moth jogged down to the communication room. He tuned the communicator to his special frequency and contacted Owl Boy, explaining what he needed.

"Let me know when you're ready and I'll drop the shields and beam you up."

"I'll be ready by the time you get to the transport room," replied Owl Boy.

"Roger, Moth out."

The Moth stood and walked down the corridor

30 feet and around a bend in the ship to a large door marked 'Transport'. He punched in the code to open the door and got behind a large control panel in front of a silver disk on the floor.

"Ready for transport, Owl Boy?" said The Moth into his communicator.

"Ready."

As he slid a series of levers, the silver disk started to glow and hum. The disk shone like a small sun as the form of Owl Boy appeared. As The Moth's apprentice continued to materialize, the disk dimmed until it became obsidian black. Owl Boy stepped off the disk and handed The Moth a device the size of a small phone.

"What can I do?"

"Stay out of my way. This isn't a safe place to be," said The Moth.

Without speaking another word, The Moth turned and headed out the door and back to the meeting room.

"You're welcome," said Owl Boy as the door closed behind The Moth.

Owl Boy walked out into the corridor and ran into the other heroes as they strolled toward the ship's dining facilities.

"How did you get up here? The ship is sealed up," asked Skylla.

"The Moth needed some equipment. He told me that I'm a great delivery boy. Sometimes I think that's all I'm good for."

"Nonsense. One day you'll be a valuable member of the Justice Alliance," said the Shadow Wraith with a smile.

"Thanks, Shadow," said Owl Boy.

"We were about to grab some food. Would you like to come with us?" asked Janus.

"Sure, I'm starved. I haven't eaten since-"

"EVERYONE TO THE MEETING ROOM, NOW!" the loud voice of The Moth boomed over the intercom system.

"Your master summons us."

"That's a cruel thing to say Janus... But probably true," said Owl Boy as his shoulders slumped.

Without further conversation, the group went straight to the meeting room. The Moth stood over the now uncovered body of Magnus.

"Owl Boy, come over here. The rest of you need to sit down."

"Have you ever considered not being a pompous jerk?" asked Skylla.

"Skylla, sit down and shut up," said The Moth through gritted teeth.

"You should at least respect the dead and cover Magnus back up," said Janus.

"I think it's a little late for respect now, don't you agree?"

"Why did you call us in here?" asked the Shadow Wraith.

"I've discovered who killed Magnus."

The group looked at each other.

"Please. We're all waiting. Which one of us did it?" asked Skylla.

"Not so soon. We need to run over a few things. First, it was common knowledge among us that Magnus' only weakness was Zim metal, but where to find it? It doesn't appear on Earth. So, to find the metal, someone would have to use a spaceship."

"So you're accusing me? How could I have killed him? I'm not a weapons expert nor am I stealthy enough to kill someone with Magnus' powers," retorted Janus.

"I'm not finished. Second, Zim metal is extremely difficult to work with and the craftsmanship of the blade is second to none."

"So now it's me?" asked Skylla. "I don't think I

need to enumerate the problems with that theory. Where would I even find Zim metal?"

"Still not finished. Lastly, who could stab him? Even if someone has the weapon, it's not like Magnus would sit still while someone stabbed him to death. That would take stealth."

"So now I am the accused," responded the Shadow Wraith.

"Wow, first Janus, then me, and now the Shadow Wraith. You're slipping. Why not accuse yourself or Owl Boy? It sounds to me like you have nothing."

"I have everything. Not one of you killed him."

"Then what-" said Janus before being interrupted.

"You all did. Janus finds the metal. Skylla forges it into a weapon, and then the Shadow Wraith stabs him. Oh, and to top it all off, Janus hacks the computer system and renders it completely useless."

"That's a great theory, but who says it wasn't you?" asked Skylla who shifted her weight from one leg to the other.

"You've bragged for years that you could take us down if we ever turned," added Janus.

"Perhaps we should talk about this, Moth."

"Shadow Wraith, you can't influence my mind, so stop trying."

"Even if it were true, you've got to have some proof and I don't think you have any. I think you're bluffing," said Skylla.

"I don't bluff when I hold all the cards. You three think that you're so smart. You're nothing. Who built this ship? Who designed it? Who is the greatest detective and crime fighter ever known?" said The Moth as he paced back and forth pointing at the other heroes.

The three heroes at the table looked at themselves.

"None of you ever had me fooled," said The Moth as his eyes shifted to the side.

"Nobody's trying to fool anyone," said Skylla never taking her eyes off of The Moth.

"Owl Boy, be ready," whispered The Moth.

"There's no use in pretending anymore. He knows," said the Shadow Wraith to Janus and Skylla before turning back to The Moth, "You understand that Magnus Superior was consumed by arrogance. He was going to get rid of us. Magnus was unstable."

"Don't you think I knew that? I had been watching him for months."

"Then what's the problem?" asked Skylla.

"We're on the same side," said Janus.

"I'm on no one's side, except my own. I had a way to stop him, to incapacitate him."

"Why would you have that?" asked Janus.

"Too much power with any single individual is bad. There has to be a way to stop any of us who becomes unstable."

"Any of us? You mean all of us, don't you?" asked the Shadow Wraith.

"If need be," responded The Moth as he opened a pouch on his uniform and pulled out a small metallic object. Janus and the Shadow Wraith moved toward The Moth as Skylla slipped her hand around the hilt of her sword.

"Is that it?" asked Janus.

"Yes, it's a neural neutralizer. Owl Boy was kind enough to bring it to me. I have to tell you that I've configured it to work with your brain patterns, even yours Shadow Wraith. With one push, your minds will shut down. That's why it was foolish to kill Magnus Superior. I could have stopped him anytime it was necessary."

"Perhaps, but what if you were wrong? With that much power, he could have destroyed us all. We couldn't count on you," said the Shadow Wraith.

"You leave me no choice but to stop you all," said The Moth as he held up the box and pressed a red button on it.

The three heroes sighed when nothing happened.

"I couldn't let this happen, Moth," came the voice from behind him.

"Owl Boy?"

A look of realization crept across The Moth's face.

"I'm so sorry," said Owl Boy as he plunged a hypodermic needle into The Moth's back.

The Moth swung his arm, knocked the syringe to the ground and crouched into a fighting stance.

"You can't win," said Skylla as she leapt at The Moth.

As The Moth rolled out of the way, he threw a punch that Skylla dodged easily. The momentum of his attempted strike caused him to fall to the side of the room.

"Stay down," said the Shadow Wraith.

The fast-fading crime fighter staggered toward the Shadow Wraith and thrust his arms forward to grab him. Before he could, the Wraith became immaterial, leaving The Moth to grab onto nothing and fall to the floor. As the drug coursed through his system, The Moth pulled himself up, but the drug had slowed down his every reaction.

"Please Moth, your struggle is not necessary," pleaded Janus.

The Moth charged Janus, but the elusive alien slid to the side allowing him to crash into the wall. Picking himself up, The Moth lunged toward him again and grabbed Janus around the waist. Janus removed his arms from him and laid him down gently on the floor.

"Moth, you never understood that you are just like Magnus Superior. Left unchecked, you would have destroyed us as well," said Janus as he bowed his head, while the Shadow Wraith and Skylla placed their hand's on Owl Boy's shoulders.

"I... I... Yes, I would."

Janus closed The Moth's eyes as his breathing slowed further and further until it stopped completely.

Epilogue

Later the next day, the four heroes along with the Mayor of Logan City gathered at a press conference in front of city hall.

"At this time, Skylla would like to make a statement on the events that happened on the spaceship Freedom, the headquarters of the Justice Alliance," said the Mayor.

"Thank you, Madam Mayor."

"As many of you know, Magnus Superior was brutally murdered last night. Janus, Shadow Wraith, Owl Boy, and myself were on the ship with The Moth, investigating the crime. Over the last few years, The Moth had unfortunately transformed from a force for justice into a dark vigilante. He became what he had sworn to fight. I'm sad to announce that The Moth murdered Magnus Superior. As a consequence, when we tried to apprehend him and get him the help he so badly needed, The Moth chose to commit suicide. It's doubly sad that we have determined that he was insane and had no idea that what he was doing was wrong. He was as much of a victim as Magnus Superior. That's all the prepared statement I have for today. I can't reveal much more than that, but are there any questions?"

A man in the front row stood up.

"Sam Jenkins, from the United Press Associates. As you know, The Moth was primarily concerned with patrolling Logan City. Regardless of his methods, he was very effective. What will happen now?"

"I'm glad you asked that. Through this trying time, there was one bright spot that shone through. I would like to ask our newest member, Owl Boy, if he would like to say something?"

Owl Boy came out from the back of the group and stepped behind the microphone.

"Thank you, Skylla. I'm not very good at public speaking, but I would like to say a few things to the good citizens. Logan City is my home and I will continue to do everything I can to protect it from evil. The events of the last few days have changed me. No mere <u>boy</u> can keep the city from those who would do it harm. As of today, Owl Boy is no more. Criminals in Logan City will now fear The Avenging Owl."

Check out my Amazon Author
Page at:

http://www.amazon.com/
Ashley-Sherer/e/
B00QCAZGUG/